OLIVER

Based on *The Railway Series* by the Rev. W. Awdry

Illustrations by
Robin Davies and Jerry Smith

EGMONT

First published in Great Britain 2004
by Egmont Books Limited
239 Kensington High Street, London W8 6SA
All Rights Reserved

Thomas the Tank Engine & Friends

A BRITT ALLCROFT COMPANY PRODUCTION

Based on The Railway Series by The Rev W Awdry

© Gullane (Thomas) LLC 2004

ISBN 1 4052 1038 9
5 7 9 10 8 6

Printed in Great Britain

This is a story about Oliver the Great Western Engine. His owner didn't want him any more and he was going to be turned into scrap. Until someone came to the rescue …

One day, Edward was talking to Douglas. They had heard that steam engines were being put out of service across the Island and replaced by new diesel engines.

"They're being turned into scrap," said Edward quietly.

"Don't mention that word!" Douglas gasped. "It makes my wheels wobble."

"I agree," replied Edward. "But The Fat Controller says he will make sure there are always steam engines on his Railway."

"I'm glad we work for The Fat Controller," smiled Douglas.

That night, Douglas was still working. He had taken the Midnight Goods Train to a station at a far away part of the Island, where only the diesels worked. He was just shunting ready for his return journey, when he heard a faint hiss.

"That sounds like a steam engine," he thought in surprise.

The hiss came again.

"Who's there?" asked Douglas.

"I'm Oliver," whispered a voice. "Are you one of The Fat Controller's engines?"

"Aye, and proud of it," replied Douglas.

"Thank goodness!" said the voice. In the darkness, Douglas could just make out a little Western Engine. "This is my coach, Isabel and brake van, Toad," said the engine. "We've run out of coal and I have no more steam."

"But, what are you doing here?" asked Douglas.

"Escaping from the scrap yard," replied Oliver, trembling.

Douglas shivered. "I'll be glad to help you," he said. "We'll make it look as though you're ready for scrap and I'm taking you away."

The Driver and Fireman agreed to help, too. Everyone worked fast. They took off Oliver's side-rods, wrote out transit labels saying that he belonged to The Fat Controller, and chalked 'SCRAP' all over him.

"Nay time for me to turn around," panted Douglas. "I will have to run backwards."

Douglas and Oliver started out on their journey. But before they could leave the station, they were stopped.

"Aha!" exclaimed a Foreman, shining his torch at Oliver. "A Great Western Engine!" His light flickered further back. "With a Western coach, and a brake van! You can't take these."

"But they're all for us. See for yourself," exclaimed Douglas' Driver.

Douglas' Driver showed him the transit labels. Oliver and Douglas hardly dared to breathe.

The Foreman looked all over Oliver.
"Seems in order. You can go, Driver," he said.

"Phew! That was a near thing," puffed Douglas.

"We've had worse," smiled Oliver. "We were nearly caught getting here and had to hide on an old quarry branch for three days. I was very frightened."

"I'm not surprised," replied Douglas. And they forged ahead.

It was daylight when their journey ended.

"We're home!" cried Douglas as they reached The Fat Controller's Railway. "I know just the place for you." And he showed them an empty siding, nicely hidden away.

"Goodbye and thank you," whispered Oliver.

"I was happy to help," smiled Douglas, and he puffed away.

Back at the shed, Douglas told the other engines all about Oliver. They were very excited, and agreed that something must be done for him.

"The Fat Controller will have to know," said James.

"Douglas should tell him at once," added Gordon firmly.

"Well, here I am," said a cheerful voice. "Now, what's all this about?"

It was The Fat Controller! The engines were silent.

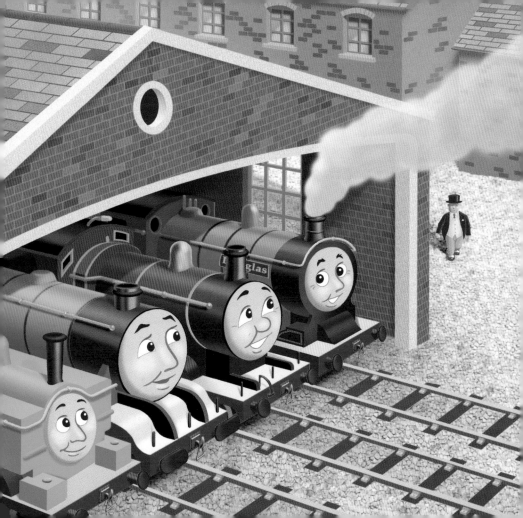

"Beg your pardon, Sir, but we do need another engine," said Duck quietly, at last.

"Yes Sir, a steam engine Sir," said Gordon.

"We do indeed!" replied The Fat Controller.
"But I'm afraid that unless one is saved from scrap, there's little hope."

"But Sir," burst out Douglas, "one has been!"

"Who told you that, Douglas?" asked The Fat Controller.

The engines looked nervously at each other.

"Sir, er … I saved him," muttered Douglas.

"You saved a steam engine?" exclaimed The Fat Controller. "I want to hear everything!"

So Douglas told him all about how he had rescued Oliver, Isabel and Toad from the scrap yard. When he had finished, The Fat Controller smiled.

"I'm proud of you, Douglas," he said. "Oliver, Isabel and Toad are just what we need for Duck's branch line."

"Thank you, Sir!" replied Douglas.

And all the engines cheered.

The Fat Controller soon had Oliver, Isabel and Toad mended and painted in full Great Western colours. They are very happy on Duck's branch line.

As Oliver puffs along the coast, he often thinks about what a lucky escape he had. If Douglas hadn't come to the rescue things would be very different. Oliver is very grateful to Douglas and everyone at The Fat Controller's Railway for his lovely new home!

The Thomas Story Library is THE definitive collection of stories about Thomas and ALL his Friends.

You can buy the Collector's Pack containing the first ten books for £24.99!

ISBN 1 4052 0827 9

5 more Thomas Story Library titles will be chuffing into your local bookshop in September 2005:

Trevor

Bertie

Diesel

Daisy

Spencer

And there are even more Thomas Story Library books to follow later!

So go on, start your Thomas Story Library NOW!

A Fantastic Offer for Thomas the Tank Engine Fans!

STICK
POUND
COIN
HERE

In every Thomas Story Library book like this one, you will find a special token. Collect 6 Thomas tokens and we will send you a brilliant Thomas poster, and a double-sided bedroom door hanger!

Simply tape a £1 coin in the space above, and fill out the form overleaf.

TO BE COMPLETED BY AN ADULT

To apply for this great offer, ask an adult to complete the coupon below and send it with a pound coin and 6 tokens, to:
THOMAS OFFERS, PO BOX 715, HORSHAM RH12 5WG

☐ Please send a Thomas poster and door hanger. I enclose 6 tokens plus a £1 coin. (Price includes P&P)

Fan's name...

Address...

....Postcode.............................

Date of birth...

Name of parent/guardian..

Signature of parent/guardian..

Please allow 28 days for delivery. Offer is only available while stocks last. We reserve the right to change the terms of this offer at any time and we offer a 14 day money back guarantee. This does not affect your statutory rights.

☐ Data Protection Act: If you do not wish to receive other similar offers from us or companies we recommend, please tick this box. Offers apply to UK only.

Cut along the dotted line